This true story happened to my brother.
It is written as he told it to me; Junior was certain
that he had met God. Soon everyone believed he did
and my brother became a legend on Green Street.
Junior changed that day but so did everyone on Green Street.

–JSG

A Voice as Soft as a Honey Bee's Flutter

Text and illustrations © 2019 by Jan Spivey Gilchrist

Discovery House is affiliated with Our Daily Bread Ministries, Grand Rapids, Michigan.

Requests for permission to quote from this book should be directed to:
Permissions Department, Discovery House, PO Box 3566, Grand Rapids, MI 49501
or contact us by email at permissionsdept@dhp.org.

Scriptures taken from the Holy Bible, New International Reader's Version®, NIrV®. Copyright © 1995, 1996, 1998, 2014 by Biblica, Inc.™ Used by permission of Zondervan. www.zondervan.com The "NIrV" and "New International Reader's Version" are trademarks registered in the United States Patent and Trademark Office by Biblica, Inc.™

Interior design by Kris Nelson/StoryLook Design

Library of Congress Cataloging-in-Publication Data

Names: Gilchrist, Jan Spivey, author.
Title: A voice as soft as a honey bee's flutter / by Jan Spivey Gilchrist.
Description: Grand Rapids : Discovery House, 2019.
Identifiers: LCCN 2019006359 | ISBN 9781627079365 (hardcover)
Subjects: LCSH: Spivey, Charles, d. 2017—Juvenile literature. | Christian
children—Biography—Juvenile literature. | Spiritual llife—Christianity—Juvenile literature.
Classification: LCC BR1715.S65 G55 2019 | DDC 277.3/082092 [B] —dc23

Printed in USA

First printing in 2019

A Voice as Soft as a Honey Bee's Flutter

Inspired by
Psalm 46

JAN SPIVEY GILCHRIST

Discovery House®
from Our Daily Bread Ministries

Junior was the preacher's son. At an early age, a voice as soft as a honey bee's flutter spoke to him. The voice knew his heart, calmed his spirit, and made him strong every day and everywhere. But it also made him different. He was born in the middle between Jan, Gail, Loonie, and Duckie.

Because Junior wasn't like his sisters, or much like other children, he found himself in trouble most of the time.

His sisters said he was made of snakes and snails.
When his heart raced and his spirit raised, anger would
begin to creep inside. The voice would whisper,

"BE STILL...BE STILL..."

His father gave him special time. Junior told his
father about the voice, and his father understood.

He read to Junior every night from the Bible. Soon Junior memorized his favorite Bible verses and recited them for his sisters. But his sisters never listened. And the voice whispered,

"BE STILL...
BE STILL..."

Junior still wanted to play with his sisters.
So he tried and tried, but he just couldn't fit in.

One day, while reciting Bible verses to himself, Junior
found children listening, and then following him each day.

Soon Junior felt proud to be like his father. He felt so proud that he forgot to listen to the voice. He thought he didn't need to. The voice whispered,

"BE STILL...BE STILL..."

Thunder roared and lightning struck and frightened away the children.

Junior's heart raced and his spirit raised and anger took over.

He felt snakes and snails covering his body. He ran out and stood in the rain to wash them away. And the voice whispered,

"BE STILL...BE STILL..."

Junior's sisters had been afraid of storms, but he would always protect them. Now they just wanted to find their brother. He might have been different, but everyone could always depend on him. But he was nowhere to be found.

Everyone on Green Street searched for Junior well into the night.

Never giving up, his father returned to the backyard. His mother and sisters followed. And there in the garden sat Junior.

When his father asked him where he had been, Junior whispered,

"I was with God."

"The voice said, 'Come to the water.'"

His father asked, "Weren't you afraid?"

Junior answered, "I knew the voice.
I didn't know who he was, but now I know.
He said,

'BE STILL AND
KNOW THAT I AM GOD.'"

This book is based on Psalm 46:1, 4, 7, 10

God is our place of safety. He gives us strength.

He is always there to help us in times of trouble.

God's blessings are like a river.

The LORD who rules over all is with us.

He says, "Be still, and know that I am God."

Read more about knowing God in Psalms 2:12c; 24:10; and 47:2.

Junior (Charles Spivey Jr.) grew up, married, became a father of four children, and fought in the Vietnam War. He was injured, and lived a normal life. He is buried in Abraham Lincoln National Cemetery in Illinois with his father, the Reverend Charles Spivey Sr. Junior was a loving brother until he died of diabetes in October 2017.